POIKO
QUESTS & STUFF
WONDERBOUND

POIKO
QUESTS & STUFF

BRIAN MIDDLETON

WRITTEN & ILLUSTRATED BY
Brian Middleton

EDITED BY **Rebecca Taylor**
DESIGNED BY **Sonja Synak**

PUBLISHER, **Damian A. Wassel**
EDITOR-IN-CHIEF, **Adrian F. Wassel**
SENIOR ARTIST, **Nathan C. Gooden**
MANAGING EDITOR, **Rebecca Taylor**
DIRECTOR OF SALES & MARKETING, DIRECT MARKET, **David Dissanayake**
DIRECTOR OF SALES & MARKETING, BOOK MARKET, **Syndee Barwick**
PRODUCTION MANAGER, **Ian Baldessari**
ART DIRECTOR, WONDERBOUND, **Sonja Synak**
ART DIRECTOR, VAULT, **Tim Daniel**
PRINCIPAL, **Damian A. Wassel Sr.**

WONDERBOUND
Missoula, Montana,
readwonderbound.com
@readwonderbound

ISBN: 978-1-63849-071-5
LCCN: 2021922757

First Edition, First Printing, March, 2022
1 2 3 4 5 6 7 8 9 10

Printed in USA

For my wonderful wife, Meghan, and my lovely daughters, Isabel and Penelope. Being with you is my favorite thing.

Delivery: **1**

LOOKS LIKE IT'S TIME TO GO TO WORK, KENSIE. WHAT'S ON THE DOCKET?!
WELL, THESE PACKAGES NEED TO GO TO THE CAT MAGE WHO LIVES ON THE OTHER SIDE OF NEVERFIELD WOODS.
I SPENT ALL MORNING PLANNING THE PERFECT ROUTE. THEN I PACKED YOUR LUNCH AND PUT IT IN YOUR POCKET, JUST HOW YOU LIKE.
WE SHOULD BE ABLE TO DELIVER ON-TIME EASY-PEASY IF WE JUST **STAY FOCUSED.**
HERE WE GO, HERE WE GO! MEET **POIKO** (THE LION) AND **KENSIE** (THE BAT)! THEY WORK TOGETHER AT **POIKO'S QUESTS AND STUFF!**
BMZ

I FEEL LIKE WHEN YOU'RE SAYING "WE" YOU ACTUALLY MEAN **ME**, PAL.
YOU **DO** HAVE A TENDENCY TO WANDER OFF OF THE PLANNED PATH, POIKO.
IT'S ONE OF THE THINGS I LOVE ABOUT YOU.
BUT I'D LOVE YOU EVEN **MORE** IF OUR PUNCTUALITY RATING WAS HIGHER THAN ONE OUT OF FOUR STARS!

INTO
THE WOODS
WE GO...

MAN...

I LOVE
THIS JOB!

I LOVE THAT TREE. IT'S SO TALL!
WAIT... DO YOU HEAR THAT?
SURE DO! DO YOU SEE THAT SMALL PERSON OVER THERE WAVING HER ARMS?
HELP!!

I DO.
IT LOOKS LIKE SHE IS IN TROUBLE!
REMEMBER, WE'RE STAYING FOCUSED TODAY...

I REMEMBER.
I'LL FOCUS UP AGAIN AS SOON AS I FINISH HELPING.
WELP... GOODBYE ONE-STAR RATING...HELLO NO STARS.

HEY! WHAT'S THE PROBLEM? ARE YOU HURT? IN DANGER?
SAUNDERS
NOT ME! IT'S MY FATHER, ACHILLES.
HE CLIMBED THAT GIANT TREE THIS MORNING AND HASN'T COME BACK YET.

DO YOU THINK YOU COULD FLY UP AND GET HIM, MR. BAT?
I'D GO UP, BUT HE SAID IF I EVEN THINK OF CLIMBING THAT TREE I'D BE GROUNDED FOR LIFE!

WHAT DO YOU SAY, KENS?
YOU KNOW I'M AFRAID OF HEIGHTS!
SAUNDE

I'M GOING TO NEED YOU TO WATCH THE PACKAGES THEN, BUD.
YOU'RE GOING UP AFTER HIM?

I KNOW YOU WANT OUR ON-TIME DELIVERY RATING UP, BUT YOU KNOW HOW I FEEL.
IF WE HAVE IT IN OUR POWER TO HELP SOMEONE, I BELIEVE WE SHOULD.
YOU WOULDN'T BE YOU IF YOU DIDN'T GO AND HELP, POIKO.
DOES THAT MEAN YOU ARE GOING TO CLIMB UP THERE?

I CAN'T BELIEVE I'M SAYING THIS, BUT...YES. YES, I AM.
BE CAREFUL UP THERE.
AND BE QUICK IF YOU CAN.
MAYBE WE COULD STILL BE ON TIME IF YOU HURRY.

I'LL TRY MY BEST, BUDDY!
MAYBE YOU COULD RELAX A LITTLE AND JAM ON THAT HARMONICA HOW YOU LIKE.
GOOD CALL, POIKO. NOTHING CALMS MY NERVES LIKE A LITTLE PUNK ROCK!

OH BOY.

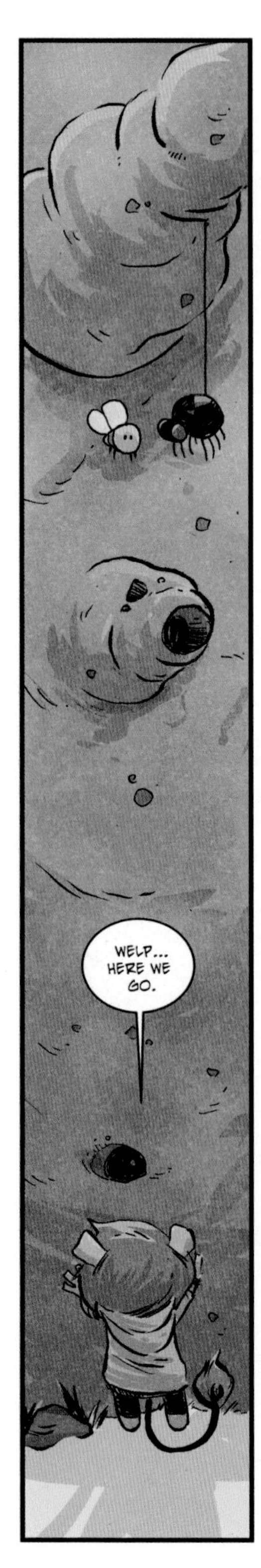
WELP... HERE WE GO.

~HRNT~

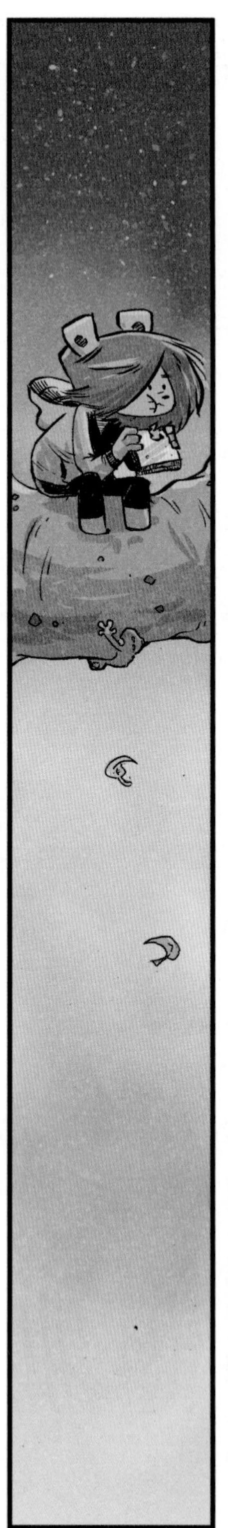

COME ON UP.
ARE YOU INTERESTED IN SOME COFFEE? IT'S NICE AND HOT!

THANKS!
I'M POIKO! IT'S NICE TO MEET YOU.
A PLEASURE TO MEET YOU, POIKO.
MY NAME IS ACHILLES.

~GLUG~
~GLUG~

WHOA! THAT'S DELICIOUS! NICE AND HOT, JUST LIKE YOU SAID.
I HAVE MANY FLAWS. BUT I'D NEVER LIE ABOUT COFFEE.

SO, UH, YOUR DAUGHTER SENT ME UP HERE TO CHECK ON YOU.
I DIDN'T MEAN TO SCARE HER. I JUST NEEDED SOME AIR.

I'VE HAD A ROUGH GO OF IT, LATELY.
WHEN MY GRANDFATHER PASSED AWAY I COULD SEE HOW MUCH IT BUMMED OUT MY DAD.
AND ALL I CAN THINK ABOUT IS HOW SAD MY DAUGHTER WILL BE WHEN I'M GONE.
IT'S ALL I CAN THINK ABOUT.
SHE KEEPS ASKING ME TO TEACH HER GUITAR, BUT I CAN'T FOCUS ON ANYTHING.
IT'S TERRIFYING!

JEEZ.
I'M NOT REALLY SURE WHAT TO SAY, OR EVEN HOW I WOULD HANDLE SOMETHING LIKE THAT.
IT MUST BE VERY DIFFICULT.
I'M SORRY FOR YOUR LOSS.
IT SOUNDS LIKE YOUR GRANDFATHER WAS REALLY LOVED.
MY GRANDFATHER USED TO SAY THAT IT'S NOT "IF" SORROW COMES, BUT "WHEN".
AND ON THAT DAY IT DOES COME, YOU CAN LET IT DRAG YOU DOWN. OR...
YOU CAN CHOOSE JOY.

I GUESS I HAD THE ANSWER ALL ALONG. MY PAP SURE WAS A SMART COOKIE.
I APPRECIATE YOUR HELP TODAY. SOMETIMES ALL IT TAKES TO FIGURE OUT A PROBLEM IS SOMEONE WHO WILL LISTEN.
DO YOU NEED A RIDE BACK DOWN?

WHAT?! FOR REAL? YES!

POIKOOoo
HUH?
HRMM... SOUNDS LIKE MAYBE YOU SHOULD GO ON WITHOUT ME.

COULD YOU TELL MY PAL, KENSIE, THAT I'LL JUST BE A LITTLE WHILE LONGER YET. AND THAT I'M SORRY! AND THAT I'M HURRYING!
YOU GOT IT!

IZZY!
POPPA!!

OOOOOFF!
I'M SO GLAD THAT YOU'RE SAFE! WASN'T SURE YOU WERE GUNNA COME BACK DOWN!

WHAT? AND MISS OUT ON JAMMING WITH YOU? NO WAY!
REALLY?

LET ME GRAB MY GUITAR AND I'LL GIVE YOU YOU A LESSON!
BUT FIRST, I GOTTA TELL YOU THIS:
I LOVE YOU SO MUCH, KIDDO.
I'M SORRY IF I WAS DISTANT, BUT I'M HERE FOR YOU. **ALWAYS.**
AND HEY, KENSIE, YOU'RE WELCOME TO JOIN IN. POIKO IS GOING TO BE A WHILE, YET.

I'M IN. I'M ALWAYS READY TO JAM.

WAIT. WHERE DID POIKO GO?
GREAT QUESTION, KENS! LET'S FIND OUT!

♫POIKO WILL YOU COME WITH USSS?♫
I'D LOVE TO. BUT TO WHERE?!

♫OUT AMONG THE STARS.♫
HUH?

WHAT EVEN ARE YOU?
♫POIKO WILL YOU COME WITH USSS?♫

I FEEL LIKE I SHOULD BE NERVOUS, Y'KNOW?
BUT...
♫WHETHER NEAR OR FAAAARR?♫

THIS...
IS...
AWESOME!

I'M HAVING A BLAST WITH YOU ALL.

SAME HERE!
BUT OUR TIME TOGETHER IS COMING TO AN END.

WHAT A BUMMER. I WISH YOU ALL COULD COME WITH ME.
THE BOYS AND EVE AND I HAVE HAD A GREAT TIME. MAYBE THERE IS A LESSON HERE:
"IT'S NOT THE LENGTH OF THE HANG, IT'S THE QUALITY."

SOUNDS JUST RIGHT TO ME!
WELL, TEAM, THIS LOOKS LIKE MY STOP UP AHEAD...

I HOPE TO SEE YOU AGAIN SOMEDAY!

HEY! WHO'S THAT? COME ON AND LET ME GET A LOOK AT YOU.

I'M POIKO. I RODE IN WITH SOME SPACE FISH, IF YOU CAN BELIEVE IT.

CAN'T SAY I'VE EVER EVEN HEARD OF SPACE FISH.
BUT I DO *KNOW* A GOOD BIT ABOUT SPACE.
IT'S PEACEFUL HERE. AND A GREAT PLACE TO COMPOSE MY POETRY.
BUT IT'S A LOUSY PLACE TO FIND AN AUDIENCE.

I'VE SPENT THE LAST FEW YEARS WORKING ON WHAT I CONSIDER MY BEST WORK.
ANY CHANCE *YOU* WANT TO HEAR IT?
I'D BE HONORED TO!

WHEN I WAS YOUNG, MY EYES WERE WIDE...
BECAUSE OF THAT, I SAW...
LIONS LAYING BESIDE LAMBS...
NO USE FOR TOOTH OR CLAW...

I GREW OLDER AND ASSUMED...
MY EYES WOULD SEE THE SAME...
IMAGINE MY SURPRISE TO FIND...
THE STRONG PREY ON THE LAME.

I SAW THE WORLD FOR WHAT IT WAS...
MY HEART WAS FILLED WITH SORROW...
AND CONVICTION TO CREATE...
A BRIGHT, BETTER TOMORROW.

IN THIS, WE CAN FIND MEANING:
LET'S COMPORT OURSELVES WITH GRACE...
LOVE EACH AND EVERY OTHER...
AND MAKE THE WORLD A BETTER PLACE.

WHOA.

THANKS FOR SHARING THAT WITH ME. I DON'T THINK I'LL EVER FORGET HOW THAT MADE ME FEEL.

IT MEANS THE WORLD TO ME TO HEAR YOU SAY THAT, POIKO.
IT WAS SUCH A JOY TO PERFORM THAT PIECE!
IF IT MOVED YOU, PERHAPS IT WILL ALSO MOVE OTHERS. THAT IS MY HOPE.

I'M CERTAIN THAT IT WILL, FRIEND.
I'LL REST EASY, KNOWING THAT YOU THINK SO, POIKO.

ZZZZZZZZZZ...
HUH! YOU WEREN'T KIDDING!
SLEEP WELL, OLD MAN.

HE WILL...

I'LL SEE TO THAT!

THAT'S DEFINITELY THE COOLEST BIRD I'VE EVER SEEN IN MY ENTIRE LIFE!
ZZZZZZZZZZZ...

I BET IT IS, POIKO.
I'M GLAD TO SEE THAT PIERRE WAS ABLE TO PERFORM HIS POEM.

PLEASE ACCEPT MY DEEPEST THANKS!
IT'S NO PROBLEM! I'M GLAD TO HAVE MET THIS OLD FELLA.

THIS "OLD FELLA" IS THE WORLD'S PREMIER POET.
BUT HE'S TOO STUBBORN TO GO OUT AND FIND AN AUDIENCE.

SO I ENLISTED THE SPACE FISH TO FIND A GOOD LISTENER AND BRING THEM HERE.

NEAT! I FEEL BLESSED THAT THEY PICKED ME.

BUT IT DOES LEAVE ME IN A BIT OF A PICKLE.
IS THERE ANY WAY THAT I COULD GET A RIDE HOME?

UNFORTUNATELY, MY STEED IS NOT STRONG ENOUGH TO BEAR THE WEIGHT OF THREE.
BUT IF YOU TRAVEL THROUGH THE HOLE IN THAT TREE, I BELIEVE YOU WILL FIND WHAT YOU NEED.

FARE-WELL!
IT'S VERY DARK IN THERE!
BE SURE TO BRING A LIGHT!
A LIGHT...
I DIDN'T BRING A LIGHT...

BUT REALLY, HOW DARK COULD IT BE?

WHOA.
PRETTY DARK, I GUESS.

HE TOLD ME IT WOULD BE DARK, AND I DIDN'T LISTEN.

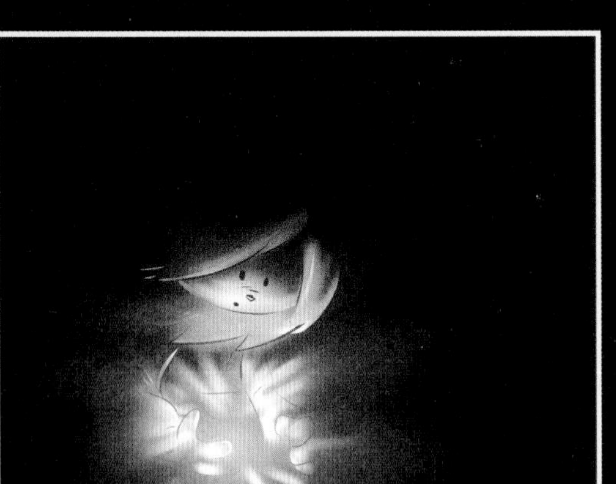

COME ALONG, FRIENDS.
OL' PHILLIP RIVERMAN KNOWS THE WAY.

IT'S ALL RIVERS FROM HERE 'TIL THE EXIT, AND I'VE GOT THE ONLY BOAT AROUND.
CAN WE GET A RIDE?
SURE CAN, BUT YOU'LL HAVE TO WAIT A BIT.
THIS IS A HUNGRY JOB, AND I FORGOT TO PACK A LUNCH.

MAN, I WISH I HAD A LUNCH TO OFFER YOU. I NEED TO GET MOVING SO I CAN KEEP MY PROMISE TO KENS.
WHAT ABOUT THAT SAMMY I SAW IN YOUR POCKET?
OH MAN, I FORGOT ALL ABOUT THAT THING! GOOD THING YOU WERE "FISHING" AROUND IN THERE!

YES. I CAN SMELL IT NOW! COLD SPAGHETTI ON BUTTERED BREAD, YES?
AND ACCEPTABLE, IF THE OFFER IS ON THE TABLE, THAT IS.

YOU GOT IT, PHIL!
EXCELLENT!

WHOA! DOES THAT BOAT HAVE LEGS AND A TAIL?
ALL THE BEST BOATS DO. AND THIS ONE IS BEST OF ALL.
IT'S TRUE! OLD PHIL WOULD NEVER LIE!

THESE RUINS...
WHAT HAPPENED HERE?
NOTHING GOOD, POIKO.
WE WERE BUSY THAT DAY, MY BOAT AND I, FERRYING FOLK ON MUCH DARKER WATERS THAN THESE.
I DON'T KNOW IF YOU'RE THE TYPE WHO PRAYS, POIKO...
BUT IF YOU ARE, YOU MIGHT PRAY THAT DAYS LIKE THESE DON'T COME AGAIN.

DON'T BE DOWNCAST, THOUGH, LITTLE SOULS...
THERE IS SOME LIGHT UP AHEAD.

MEET MY FRIENDS, REXINALD AND MS. REDRA.
♥♥AWW, THEY'RE IN LOVE!♥♥
ARE THEY BOTHERED BY THE DIFFERENCE IN THEIR SIZE?

MS. REDRA TOLD ME ONCE THAT WHEN YOU TRULY LOVE SOMEONE, YOU'LL DO WHAT'S NEEDED TO BRIDGE ANY DIFFERENCE.
I'VE ALWAYS RECKONED THOSE TO BE WORDS TO LIVE BY.

HERE WE ARE, FRIENDS!
WHO WOULD HAVE EVER THOUGHT WE'D GET SO MUCH IN EXCHANGE FOR A COLD SPAGHETTI SANDWICH?

IT'S AN EXCHANGE THAT I WOULD HAPPILY MAKE AGAIN.
IT WAS A JOY TO HANG WITH YOU BOTH.
BACK AT YOU, PHIL!

THANKS FOR SHOWING US SOMETHING BEAUTIFUL AFTER WE SAILED THROUGH THOSE RUINS.
IT'S A KINDNESS THAT I WON'T SOON FORGET.

THERE IS ALWAYS LIGHT TO BE FOUND, POIKO, EVEN IN THE DEEPEST DARK. WE NEED ONLY LOOK TO FIND IT.
I WISH YOU SAFE TRAVELS, MY FRIENDS.

WHAT DO YOU THINK, EVE? IS THERE ALWAYS LIGHT TO BE FOUND?
I SURE HOPE SO. THERE'S PLENTY HERE AT THE END OF THIS TUNNEL!

MAN...

I LOVE THIS JOB!

KENSIE?!
POIKO!

HOW DID YOU FIND US?
I USED ECHO-LOCATION.

WHAT? REALLY?

JUST KIDDING. I PICKED A SPOT ON THE MAP AND HOPED FOR THE BEST.

NOW, COME ON. WE'VE GOT JUST ENOUGH TIME TO MAKE OUR DELIVERY.
LET'S DO THIS!

WE MADE IT!
JUST IN THE NICK OF TIME, TOO!

IT'S MY FAULT WE DIDN'T GET HERE SOONER, CAT MAGE.
I MADE A FEW STOPS ALONG THE WAY.

PLEASE DON'T BE MAD. HE WAS HELPING PEOPLE.
IT'S TRUE! I WAS THERE FOR SOME OF IT!

OH, I KNOW WHAT HE WAS UP TO. WORD TRAVELS FAST IN THESE PARTS.

I COULD NEVER BE MAD AT HIM FOR HELPING OTHERS.
I'D TAKE KINDNESS OVER AN EARLY DELIVERY ANY DAY OF THE WEEK.

WITH THEIR FINAL DELIVERY OF THE DAY COMPLETE, OUR TRIO OF TIRED TRAVELERS STARTS THEIR WALK HOME.
SO LONG!

HOME SWEET HOME IS JUST UP AHEAD.
COME ON, I'LL RACE YOU.
I'LL CATCH UP IN A MINUTE, PAL!

WELL...
THIS IS ME.
THANKS FOR WALKING ME HOME.
I LOVED EVERY MINUTE OF IT.

DO YOU THINK WE'LL SEE EACH OTHER AGAIN?
POIKO...

YOU CAN COUNT ON IT!
~SMEK!~

MAN, THAT IS ONE CLASSY SPACE FISH...

I'M GLAD TO FINALLY BE HOME!
SORRY THAT I DIDN'T QUITE STICK TO THE PLAN TODAY, KENS.
IT'S OKAY, PAL.
I LOVE THAT YOU WANT US TO HELP EVERY-ONE.
I JUST WANT TO KEEP US ON TRACK WHILE WE DO.

THAT BALANCE IS WHAT MAKES US A GOOD TEAM.
THE BEST TEAM.

I'M EXCITED TO SEE WHAT NEW **QUESTS 'N STUFF** TOMORROW WILL BRING.

I'M EXCITED TO FIND OUT TOGETHER!

Delivery: 2

HERE WE GO AGAIN! POIKO AND KENSIE OFF ON ANOTHER ADVENTURE!
LIGHT DAY TODAY, HUH, KENS?
ONLY ONE DELIVERY!
JUST THE ONE, YEP.

AND THEN IT'S TIME TO GO CAMPING!
I HOPE YOUR MOM MAKES THOSE COOKIES LIKE SHE DID WHEN WE WERE KIDS.
I HOPE WE CAN MAKE IT TO THE CAMPSITE IN A TIMELY FASHION.

YOUR MOM WAS ALWAYS A STICKLER FOR PUNCTUALITY.
SHE'D LET YOU GET AWAY WITH JUST ABOUT ANYTHING, OTHER THAN TARDINESS.
TRUE STORY, BUDDY.
THIS WILL BE MY FIRST TIME SEEING HER SINCE I MOVED OUT. I WANT TO SHOW HER THAT I STILL KEEP GOOD TIME.

YOU'VE GOT THIS, BUDDY!
I HOPE SO.

FEELS LIKE IT'S GETTING WARMER THE HIGHER WE CLIMB.
I COULD HAVE SWORN IT WAS SUPPOSED TO BE THE OTHER WAY AROUND.

WOOF!
IT'S GETTING TOASTY NOW.

SURE IS.
I THOUGHT ABOUT TAKING MY SCARF OFF, BUT I LOOK **SO NICE** IN IT.

YOU'RE NOT WRONG, PAL!

MAN!
IT FEELS LIKE SUMMERTIME UP HERE.

COME INSIDE, LITTLE PEOPLE.
WE'RE ON THE WAY.

GOOD TO MEET YOU, LITTLE FRIENDS.
I'M PENELOPE.
IS THAT MY FATHER'S COOKING I SMELL COMING FROM YOUR PACK?
IT IS!
NICE TO MEET YOU. I'M POIKO!
AND I'M KENSIE.

WE BROUGHT SOME CARE PACKAGES FOR YOU. THEY'RE FROM YOUR PARENTS!

CAREFUL NOW, LITTLE KENSIE.
DON'T GET TOO CLOSE.

BECAUSE OF THE HEAT YOU GIVE OFF?

HA!
SURE. BUT THAT'S NOT ALL!

I HAVE TERRIBLE ALLERGIES.
I CAN ONLY BEAR BEING NEAR OTHER ANIMALS FOR A SHORT TIME.

OH, THAT'S THE WORST.
YOU MUST GET VERY LONELY.
IT SOUNDS VERY HARD.

IT ISN'T AN EASY WEIGHT TO BEAR.
I MISS MY FAMILY. AND I'M NOT ABLE TO DO WHAT I WANTED WITH MY LIFE.
I HAD HOPED TO FOLLOW IN MY PARENTS' FOOT-STEPS AND BECOME A PSYCHOLOGIST ONE DAY.
IT WOULD HAVE BEEN NICE TO BE ABLE TO PUT ALL OF THIS STUDYING TO USE HELPING OTHERS.

THAT BEING SAID, MY FAMILY SENDS THESE BOOKS AND MY FAVORITE SOUP ALONG OFTEN TO REMIND ME THAT THEY ARE HERE WITH ME IN SPIRIT.
IT MAKES SOME DAYS EASIER TO BEAR.

WE'D HUG YOU IF WE COULD, BUT IT SOUNDS LIKE THAT'S NOT A GOOD IDEA.

THE SENTIMENT IS SWEET, LITTLE POIKO, AND I APPRECIATE IT SO.
BUT YOU ARE RIGHT, IT WOULD NOT BE A GOOD IDEA.
MY ALLERGIES ARE ALREADY ACTING UP, SO, AS MUCH AS IT PAINS ME, I MUST ASK YOU TO LEAVE.

BEST MAKE IT QUICK, TOO, LITTLE PEOPLE.
YOU DON'T WANT TO BE ANYWHERE NEAR HERE WHEN I SNEEZE!
WELL, THAT WAS A BUMMER.
YOU'VE NEVER BEEN A FAN OF QUICK GOOD-BYES.

AH, CRUD. I FORGOT ABOUT THE ROPE BRIDGE.
I HATE HEIGHTS!
WHY DOES THIS HAVE TO BE THE FASTEST WAY TO MY MOM?

WE TALKED ABOUT THIS, BUD.

THERE IS LIKE ZERO CHANCE THAT THIS GOES BAD.

SEE! I TOLD YOU THIS WOULD BE FINE!
YEAH, YOU REALLY DID.

AH

SO, UH...FEEL FREE TO CORRECT ME IF I AM WRONG...
BUT THAT SOUNDED LIKE THE START OF A VERY BIG SNEEZE, RIGHT?

AH

THIS IS GOING TO BE BAD, HUH?
YES, I THINK IT IS.

AHCHOOO
AH, POOP.

KENS!
WHERE ARE YOU, BUDDY?

AH!
THERE YOU ARE.
AH, JEEZ. DID YOU PASS OUT?
YOU'RE THE ONLY BAT I KNOW WHO IS AFRAID OF HEIGHTS!

BUT IT'S ALL RIGHT, BUDDY.
I LOVE YOU JUST THE WAY YOU ARE.

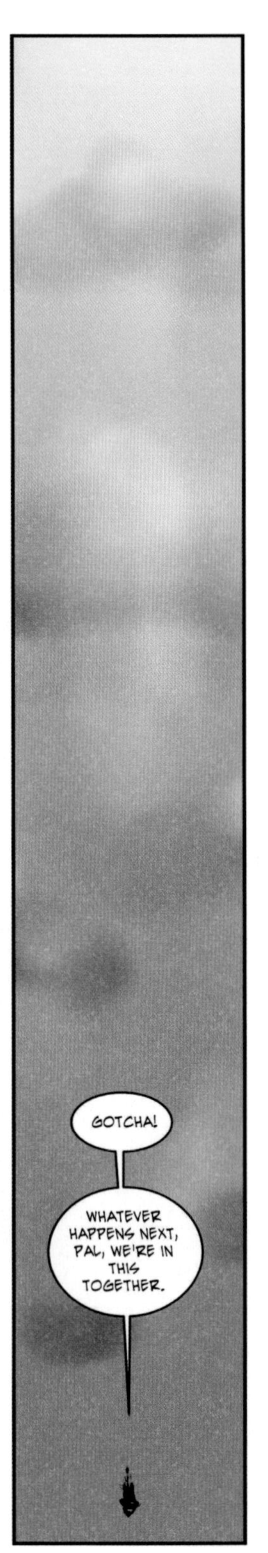
GOTCHA!
WHATEVER HAPPENS NEXT, PAL, WE'RE IN THIS TOGETHER.

SPLOOSH

AIR!
KENSIE, WE'RE GONNA' MAKE IT AFTER ALL!

OH LOOK!

MEWMAIDS!

AND WE'RE MOVING!

I WONDER WHERE SHE IS TAKING US...
WHERE-EVER IT IS, I HOPE WE GET THERE QUICKLY.

I GOT YOU, BUDDY. BUT SOMETIMES IT'S BEST JUST TO RELAX AND ENJOY THE RIDE.

GASP!
GASP!

WHAT'S UP?
UH...
PERMISSION TO COME ABOARD?

UH, SURE...
DO WHAT YOU WILL.

AND WE'RE MOVING!
YOU NOTICED THAT, HUH?

THE ONLY PROBLEM IS, WE'RE HEADED IN THE **WRONG DIRECTION!**

I DIDN'T REALIZE IT WHEN WE WERE UNDER WATER, BUT WE ARE WAY OFF COURSE.

WE'RE GOING TO BE SO LATE.
DO YOU THINK YOU SHOULD TALK TO THE CAPTAIN ABOUT TAKING US TO MY MOTHER?

I DUNNO. SHE DOESN'T SEEM TO BE IN THE MOOD TO TALK.

I AGREE. SHE SEEMS BUMMED...

BUT LET'S CHECK ANYWAY. I DON'T WANT TO BE LATE!
SIGH
OKAY, BUD.

HEY, UH, WE JUST WANTED TO SAY "THANKS" FOR LETTING US COME ABOARD.
AND...
I HEARD YOU TALKING OVER THERE.

YOU DID?
UH...

IT'S NOT A VERY BIG BOAT.

YOU WERE RIGHT, BY THE WAY.
I AM BUMMED.
AND I HAVEN'T WANTED TO TALK.

YOU SEE...
MY FATHER RECENTLY PASSED AWAY.

"MY FATHER WAS THIS WORLD'S DEFENDER AND SUPREME BATTLER.

"THE VERY DEFINITION OF THE WORD 'HERO'.

"BUT HIS WORK WAS OFTEN VIOLENT, AND I COULD NOT STAND TO WATCH IT.

"SO I TOOK TO GARDENING INSTEAD AND FOUND A SIMPLE JOY IN THE WORK OF PLANTING AND PRUNING."

"I WAS IN THAT GARDEN WHEN I HEARD THAT MY FATHER HAD GIVEN HIS LIFE TO DEFEAT SOME *GREAT* AND *GROWING* EVIL.

"WHEN I LEARNED THAT HE HAD PASSED HIS LEGACY ON TO ME, WELL...

YOU MUST UNDERSTAND, I HOLD MY FATHER IN THE HIGHEST REGARD.
HE DID MUCH TO ENSURE THE SAFETY OF KING AND COUNTRY.
AND MY SAFETY.

BUT HIS LIFE OF VIOLENCE IS **NOT** THE ONE I WANT FOR MYSELF.

I GO NOW TO THE PLACE WHERE HE LAID DOWN HIS LIFE.
I HOPE TO FIND A WAY TO HONOR HIS LEGACY WITHOUT SACRIFICING MY OWN DREAMS.
THAT'S HEAVY.

I WISH THERE WAS SOME WAY THAT WE COULD HELP YOU, VIOLETTE.

WOULD YOU...
COULD YOU COME WITH ME?

WAIT, WHAT?

I KNOW I'M STRONG ENOUGH TO BEAR THIS BURDEN ALONE...
BUT IT WOULD BE EASIER WITH FRIENDS.

BUT...
POIKO, WE HAVE A DEADLINE TO MEET.
KENS.

I LOVE YOU, AND I'LL SUPPORT HOW-EVER YOU WANNA GO HERE...

YEAH?

ALWAYS.
I KNOW HOW MUCH YOU WANT TO SHOW YOUR MOM THAT YOU ARE STILL AS RELIABLE AS EVER...
BUT WE HAVE AN OPPORTUNITY HERE TO ACTUALLY **BE** RELIABLE.
I THINK YOU MIGHT REGRET IT IF WE DON'T TAKE IT.

YEAH...
I THINK YOU MIGHT BE RIGHT.

BUT LET'S BE QUICK ABOUT IT, IF WE CAN!
COUNT US IN, VIOLETTE!
GLADLY!

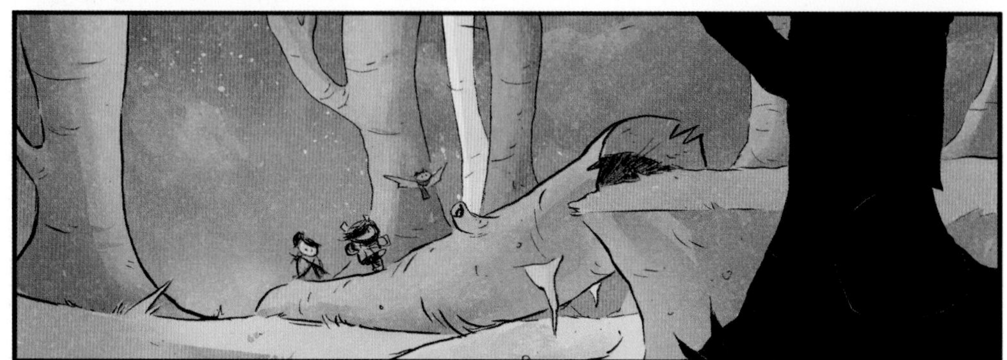

HEY, TRAVELERS!

MOST FOLKS WHO WANDER THIS WAY ARE LOST, BUT YOU'RE A GROUP THAT HAS THE FEEL OF PURPOSE ABOUT YOU.
MIGHT I HAZARD A GUESS THAT YOU'VE COME TO SEE THE SPOT WHERE AURIONUS LAID DOWN HIS LIFE FIGHTING THAT GREAT AND GROWING EVIL?

IT IS AS YOU SAY. HE WAS MY FATHER, AND I SEEK TO HONOR HIS PASSING.

I THOUGHT I RECOGNIZED HIS MIGHTY SWORD UPON YOUR BACK!
AURIONUS WAS WORTHY OF HONOR, TO BE SURE.

I WARN YOU, THOUGH, THIS FOREST IS NOT FOR THE CASUAL HIKER.
THE UNDERGROWTH IS FULL OF MENACE AND WOULD VEX EVEN THE HEARTIEST OF ADVENTURERS.

THE ONLY TRUE SAFE PLACE IS AT THE CENTER OF THE FOREST, IN THE VERY SPOT WHERE AURIONUS LAID DOWN HIS LIFE.
IF YOU ARE GOING TO THAT PLACE, BEST TO GET THERE QUICKLY. THE FOREST CLAIMS THOSE WHO DAWDLE.

YEESH! THIS IS CRAZY! "UNDERGROWTH." MORE LIKE "OVERGROWTH"!

YOU SAID IT! PLUS, IT'S GETTING DARKER THE FARTHER WE GO IN!

WOOF! THIS IS TAKING FOREVER!
SURE IS!

HOPEFULLY, IT WON'T BE MUCH--

--FARTHER...
WHOA.
VIOLETTE, YOU'VE GOT TO SEE THIS.

I THINK WE'RE HERE.

OH, PAPA...
I'VE MISSED YOU.

WHY
DID YOU LEAVE
THIS BURDEN
FOR ME?

I'M
NOT WISE OR
STRONG IN THE
SAME WAYS
YOU WERE.
I'M
NOT SURE
THAT I'M ANYTHING
LIKE YOU.

I
JUST DON'T
UNDERSTAND.

VIOLETTE, ARE YOU OKAY?
HMM?
OH, POIKO. YES, YES, I'M OKAY.

I WANT TO SAY THANK YOU FOR COMING WITH ME.
I'M NOT SURE I COULD HAVE DONE THIS ON MY OWN.

I DON'T BELIEVE THAT FOR A SECOND.
YOU'RE SO STRONG, AND YOU'RE BEARING THIS TERRIBLE BURDEN SO WELL.
I'M SURE YOUR FATHER WOULD BE PROUD.

YOU'RE A GOOD EGG, POIKO.
I'M GLAD I AGREED TO RESCUE YOU.

AGREED.
IF THERE IS ANYTHING ELSE WE CAN DO TO HELP, PLEASE LET US KNOW.
DON'T BE RIDICULOUS. YOU'VE DONE SO MUCH ALREADY.
PLUS, IT'S ALMOST NIGHTTIME, AND YOU HAVE PLACES TO BE...
IT'S TIME FOR YOU BOYS TO BE MOVING ON.

I CAN'T BELIEVE WE'RE HEADING BACK INTO THAT MESS.
THERE'S NOTHING FOR IT, BUDDY. IT'S THE ONLY WAY FORWARD.

I GUESS WE'VE GOT TO DO WHAT WE'VE GOT TO DO TO MAKE IT TO MY MOM IN TIME.
RIGHT.

HRNT.
THE GRASS IS WAY TOUGHER NOW.
RRRRR

I THINK WE'RE GOING TO HAVE TO TRY AND CUT OUR WAY THROUGH.
DID WE BRING ANYTHING SHARP?

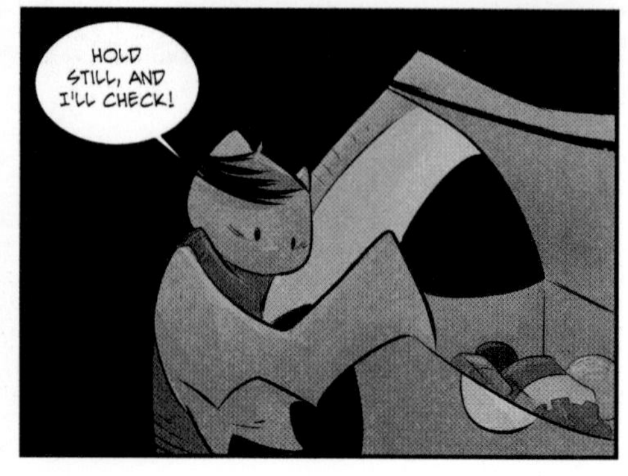
HOLD STILL, AND I'LL CHECK!

LET'S SEE...
BUTTER KNIFE...
SCISSORS...
COPING SAW...
BOX CUTTER...
BEARD TRIMMER...
WEED WACKER...
COMPOUND MITER SAW...
LET ME TRY THE WEED WACKER!

OH MAN!

KENS! IT'S NOT WORKING!

I TRIED THE SCISSORS, THE BEARD TRIMMER, AND MACHETE, AND THEY WON'T CUT EITHER!
PLUS, CALL ME CRAZY, BUT IT LOOKS LIKE IT'S GROWING!

I DON'T THINK YOU'RE CRAZY, BUD.
IT'S DEFINITELY GROWING!
WHOA!

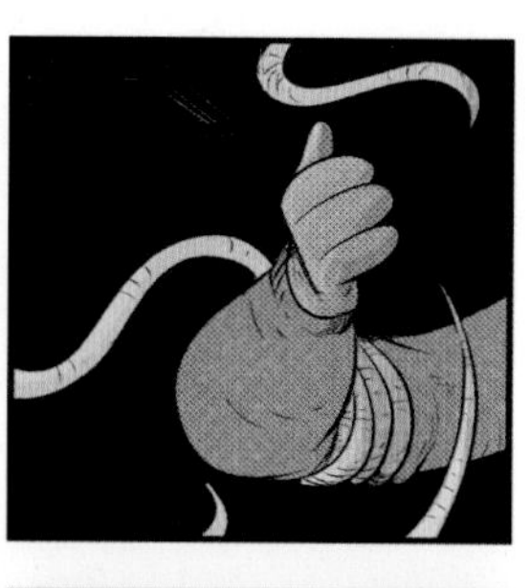

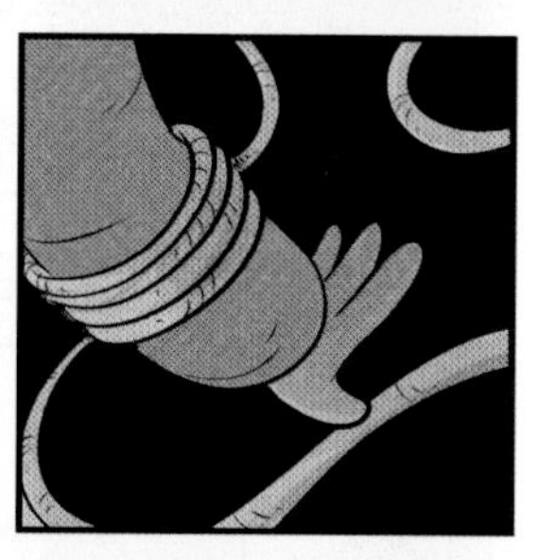

YOU REMEMBER WHEN VIOLETTE SAID THAT HER DAD HAD CONTAINED A GREAT AND GROWING EVIL?
YOU DON'T THINK...?

THIS THING IS DEFINITELY GROWING, SO YEAH, I DO THINK!

OOF! IT'S SQUEEZING ME!
~HRNT~ ME, TOO, BUD!

IT'S NOT LOOKING TOO GOOD FOR US HERE.
I WANT YOU TO KNOW, IT'S BEEN A GREAT LIFE WITH YOU BY MY SIDE, BUDDY!

IT REALLY HAS.
I'M SORRY ABOUT THAT TIME I STOPPED TALKING TO YOU FOR TWO WEEKS BECAUSE YOU BOUGHT ~HRNT~ A COUNTRY RECORD.

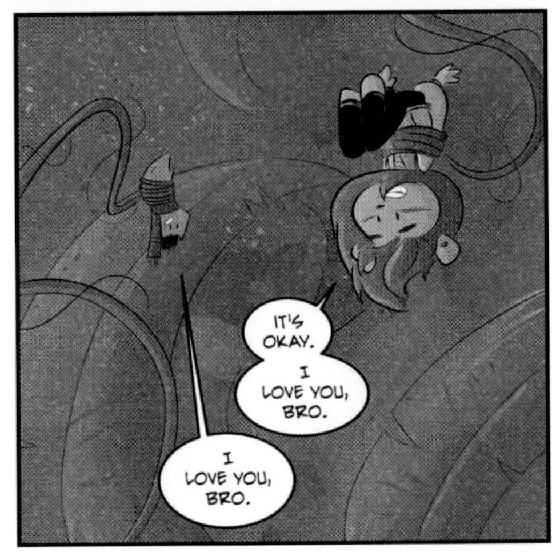
IT'S OKAY.
I LOVE YOU, BRO.
I LOVE YOU, BRO.

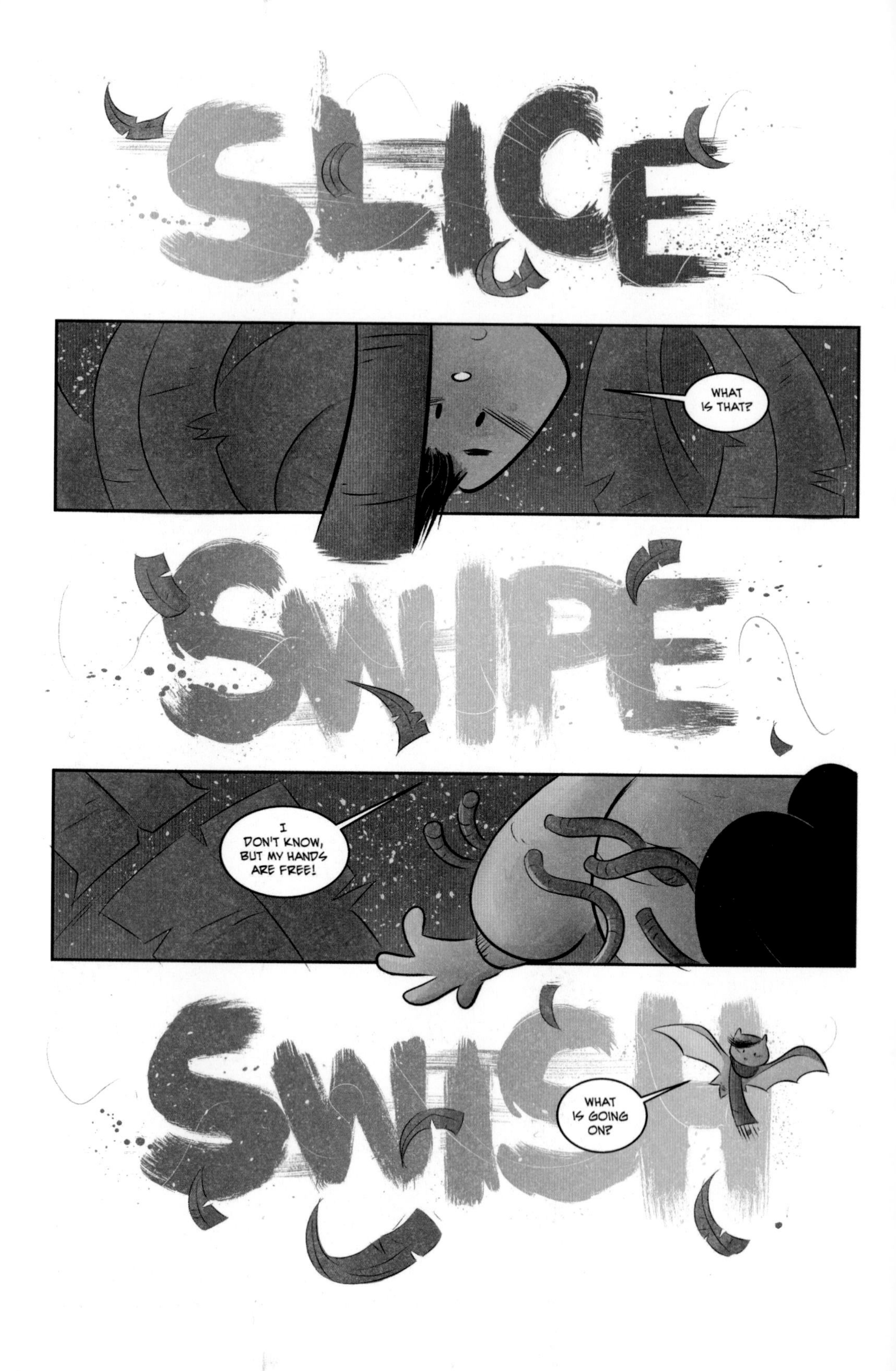
SLICE
WHAT IS THAT?
SWIPE
I DON'T KNOW, BUT MY HANDS ARE FREE!
SWISH
WHAT IS GOING ON?

SLASH

IT WAS VIOLETTE! SHE SURE SAVED OUR DAY!
YOU SAID IT.

I COULD NEVER DO WHAT YOU DID WITH THIS SWORD, PAPA...

WHOA.
THAT'S BEAUTIFUL, VIOLETTE.

BUT I CAN TAKE WHAT YOU TAUGHT ME AND USE IT TO MAKE THIS A SAFER PLACE.

THANKS SO MUCH FOR SAVING OUR BACON JUST NOW.

WE APPRECIATE IT SO MUCH!
I'D DO IT AGAIN IN A HEARTBEAT!

IT'S SO EXCITING TO THINK THAT I'VE FOUND THE ONE PLACE ON EARTH WHERE I CAN **GARDEN** AND **SAVE THE DAY!**

I LOVE HOW YOU ARE HONORING YOUR FATHER BY USING WHAT HE TAUGHT YOU, BUT DOING IT YOUR OWN WAY.

I AGREE.
IT'S SUPER COOL!
SO ARE THE TWO OF YOU!

GOOD-BYE, VIOLETTE! THANKS AGAIN!

LOOKS LIKE VIOLETTE CLEARED A PATH FOR US.
TIME TO HUSTLE!

NO MORE DETOURS, BUDDY. WE'LL MAKE IT ON TIME, I PROMISE.

ACTUALLY...

YOU MIGHT WANT TO STOP FOR THIS...
HRM?

HELLO!
IT'S BEEN QUITE SOME TIME SINCE I'VE SEEN PEOPLE.
DO YOU HAVE TIME TO HEAR THE PLIGHT OF ONE WHO COULD USE SOME HELP?
I'D LIKE TO, SIR. BUT ACTUALLY WE ARE IN A HURRY JUST NOW.
IT'S OKAY, POIKO. LET'S HEAR HIM OUT.

IN DAYS LONG PAST, MANY STOOD WHERE YOU NOW STAND.
THIS PLACE HAS LONG BEEN SACRED FOR THOSE WHO WISH TO DISCUSS DEEP THOUGHTS.

KENS, ARE YOU SURE ABOUT THIS?
SHH. LET'S LISTEN.

BUT WHEN THE GREAT AND GROWING EVIL WAS SEALED IN THIS PLACE, I NO LONGER HAD ANYONE TO SPEAK WITH.
A DEEP THOUGHT IS A GRAND THING, BUT IT IS WORTHLESS IF IT CANNOT BE DISCUSSED.

I WOULD ASK OF YOU ONE SMALL TASK...
THE COMPLETION OF WHICH WOULD BRING ME GREAT JOY.

PLEASE, JUST SPREAD THE WORD THAT THE PATH TO THE SACRED STUDY OF ORRYN IS ONCE AGAIN TRAVERSABLE.
I HAVE MANY DEEP THOUGHTS THAT I WISH TO DISCUSS WITH THOSE OF SIMILAR MINDS AND WILL NOT FIND REST UNTIL I HAVE.

WE WILL DEFINITELY SPREAD THE WORD.
BUT I THINK I CAN DO YOU ONE BETTER. I'LL BE BACK SOON.

WONDERFUL!

I CAN TELL WHAT YOU'RE THINKING, KENS, AND IT'S A GOOD IDEA. BUT I PROMISED YOU WE'D GET TO YOUR MOM WITHOUT ANY MORE DELAYS.
I KNOW YOU DID, BUDDY. AND I APPRECIATE THAT A TON.

BUT I HAVE TO DO THIS. I'LL BE BACK SOON.

HUH.

WAY TO BE, KENS.

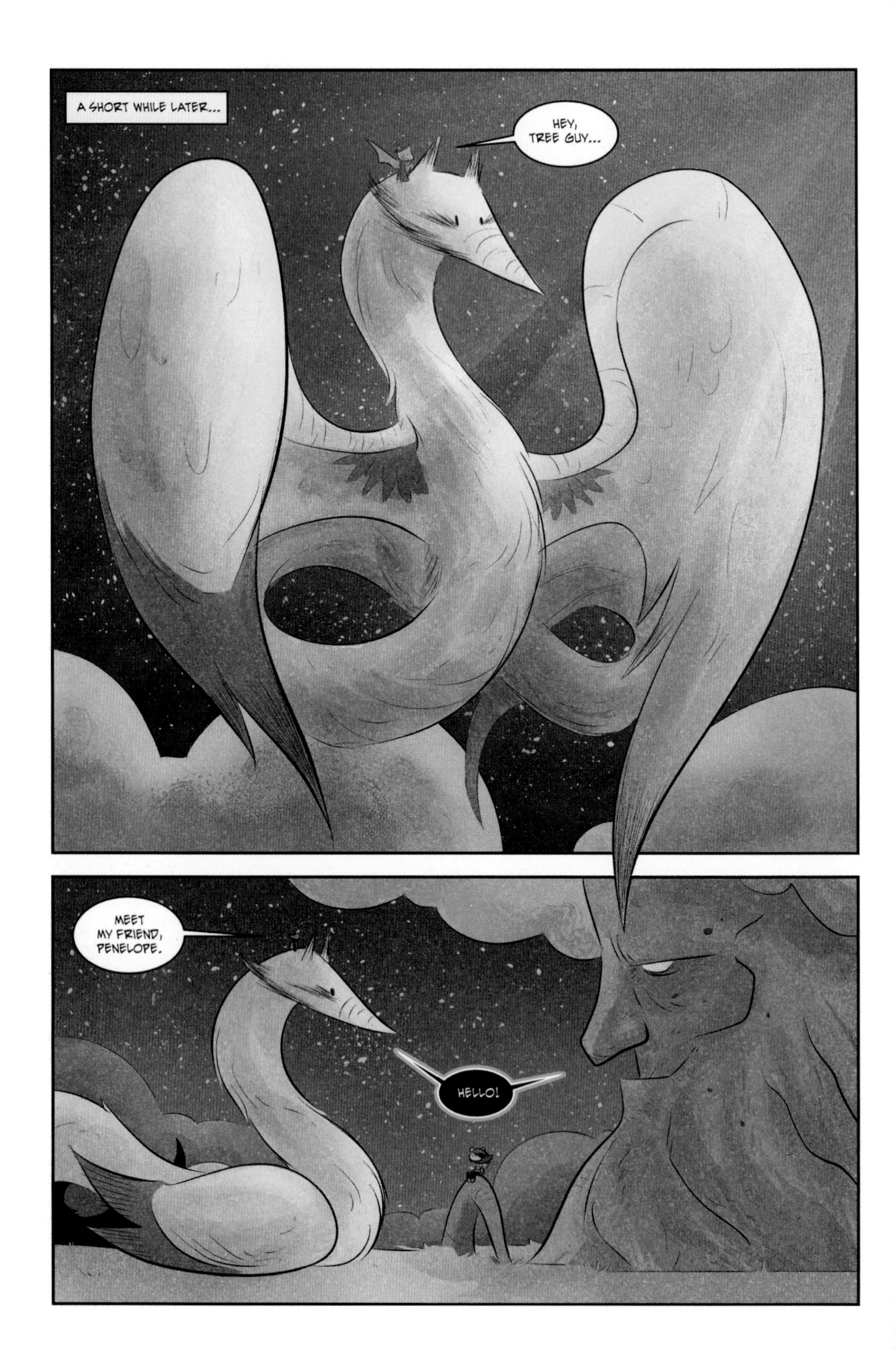
A SHORT WHILE LATER...
HEY, TREE GUY...
MEET MY FRIEND, PENELOPE.
HELLO!

IT'S A PERFECT FIT.
SHE'S A SCHOLAR WHO IS ALLERGIC TO ANIMALS, AND YOU ARE A WISE MAN IN NEED OF A DEEP THINKER TO TALK WITH.

IT DOES SOUND PERFECT, KENSINGTON.
THANK YOU FOR YOUR KINDNESS.

I UNDERSTAND THAT YOU RAN THIS ERRAND FOR ME EVEN THOUGH IT WILL MAKE YOU LATE FOR AN IMPORTANT ENGAGEMENT.
WHY WOULD YOU DO THAT?

WELL, I MET A NEW FRIEND TODAY.
HER FATHER HAD TAUGHT HER THE SKILLS THAT WERE IMPORTANT TO HIM. BUT THEY DIDN'T FIT WELL WITH THE LIFE SHE HAD IN MIND FOR HERSELF.

SHE PUT HER MIND TO IT AND FOUND A WAY TO USE THEM WHILE STILL STAYING TRUE TO WHO SHE WANTS TO BE.
IT MADE ME REALIZE THAT I DO THAT, TOO!

I USE THE SKILLS MY MOTHER TAUGHT ME EVERY DAY TO HELP POIKO MAKE OUR DELIVERIES ON TIME. OR AS CLOSE TO "ON TIME" AS POSSIBLE.
BUT TIMELINESS ISN'T THE ONLY THING THAT'S IMPORTANT TO ME. SO IS HELPING PEOPLE.
I JUST HOPE SHE UNDERSTANDS.

OF COURSE I UNDERSTAND!
HUH?

MOM!

MY DEAR, SWEET BOY! I DIDN'T TEACH YOU TO BE ON TIME ONLY FOR MY BENEFIT.
I'M ECSTATIC TO HEAR THAT YOU ARE PUTTING THOSE SKILLS TO GOOD USE FOR OTHERS.

AND WHILE I DO LOVE IT WHEN YOU ARE ON TIME, I COULD NEVER BE MAD AT YOU FOR HELPING THOSE IN NEED.

I'M SO GLAD TO HEAR THAT.
AND I'M SO GLAD YOU'RE HERE. HOW DID YOU KNOW WHERE TO FIND US ANYWAY?

POIKO CAME FOR ME WHILE YOU WERE GETTING PENELOPE.
HE TOLD ME WHAT YOU WERE DOING AND HOW YOU DREADED BEING LATE.

I FIGURED BRINGING YOUR MOM HERE WAS THE CLOSEST THING TO KEEPING MY PROMISE TO YOU.

SO, ARE WE READY TO CAMP, OR WHAT?
I AM! AND I BET PENELOPE'S ALLERGIES ARE READY FOR US TO LEAVE, TOO!
IT'S TRUE!

IN FACT, I FEEL A SNEEZE COMING ON RIGHT NOW...
AH- AH- AH-
UH OH.
YIPE!

JUST KIDDING!

GOOD ONE, PENELOPE!

Delivery: 3

I SEE POIKO! I SEE KENSIE! MUST BE TIME FOR ANOTHER ADVENTURE!
YOU KNOW WHAT I LOVE ABOUT THIS JOB, KENS?
WHAT'S THAT?

EVERYTHING!

BUT MOSTLY I LOVE HANGING WITH MY BEST PAL!

RIGHT ON, PAL. I FEEL THE SAME WAY.

MISS MANE'S PUNK ROCK EMPORIUM
SO THIS IS THE PLACE, HUH?
YEP!

THERE IS SO MUCH AWESOME GEAR IN HERE!
I KNOW! I'VE ALWAYS LOVED IT HERE.

I GUESS I SHOULDN'T BE SURPRISED THAT YOU'VE BEEN HERE BEFORE.
YOU *LOVE* PUNK ROCK!

MY DAD USED TO BRING ME HERE WHEN I WAS A TOT.

AND YOU'RE JUST AS CUTE NOW AS YOU WERE BACK THEN!

MISS MANE!
DO YOU STILL PLAY THE HARMONICA I GAVE TO YOU?
EVERY DAY.

SO GLAD TO HEAR IT!
NOW, I'M SURE YOU BOYS ARE INTERESTED TO HEAR ABOUT THE LETTER YOU ARE ABOUT TO DELIVER...

ACTUALLY, WE WERE GOING TO ASK YOU ABOUT THAT.

WE'RE HAPPY FOR THE WORK, BUT WE WERE KIND OF SURPRISED THAT YOU PICKED US TO DELIVER A LETTER.
THAT SEEMS LIKE A JOB FOR THE POST OFFICE.

THAT WOULD BE TRUE IN MOST CASES.
BUT MY FRIEND SPENDS HIS TIME DEEP WITHIN A DARK AND PERILOUS DUNGEON.
I'LL NEED A TOP-NOTCH QUESTING TEAM TO GET THE LETTER TO HIM.

TOP-NOTCH?
THAT'S US IN A NUTSHELL.

DELIVERING MAIL WHERE THE POSTFOLKS FEAR TO TREAD?
THAT'S RIGHT UP OUR ALLEY!

I KNEW I PICKED THE RIGHT TEAM FOR THE JOB!
NOW, TAKE THIS LETTER...

"...AND STAY SAFE OUT THERE IN THE BIG, BLUE WORLD!"

I'M GETTING HUNGRY.
LET'S BREAK FOR LUNCH!

MMM.
MMM.
MMM!
I DON'T KNOW HOW YOU JUST KEEP GETTING BETTER AT MAKING SAMMIES, BUT I SURE AM GLAD FOR IT!
PEANUT BUTTER AND BANANA...
TOASTED CHEESE AND SALSA...
BREAD ON BREAD...

I LOVE THEM ALL!
I COULD EAT EVERY ONE OF THESE SAMMIES RIGHT NOW!
SO GOOD!

IT'D PROBABLY BE BETTER IF YOU WAITED.
MISS MANE SAID IT MIGHT BE PERILOUS.
WE DON'T KNOW HOW LONG THIS JOB IS GOING TO TAKE.

AND THAT IS WHY YOU ARE REFERRED TO AS "THE BRAINS OF THIS OPERATION," KENS!

YOU KNOW WHAT I WAS THINKING?
?
-MUNCH- -MUNCH-

MAYBE WE COULD BRING EVE IN ON THIS ONE.
LAST TIME I WAS IN A DARK PLACE, SHE SAVED THE DAY.

SHE DEFINITELY HAS THE RIGHT SKILLS FOR THIS.
I GOTTA SAY, THOUGH, I'M NEVER SURE WHETHER I SHOULD CONSIDER HER AN ACQUAINTANCE OR A FRIEND.

I GET THAT.
SHE ISN'T AROUND THAT MUCH, IS SHE?

SHE'S REALLY BUSY. AND LIVES IN SPACE.
IT'S FINE. I'VE JUST ALWAYS THOUGHT THAT FRIENDS SHOULD TALK ALL OF THE TIME.

I GOTCHA.
EITHER WAY, I THINK SHE'LL BE GREAT FOR THIS JOB.
AGREED.

HUH. SO THIS IS IT.
I LOVE THE BUNNY DECOR!

NO SIGN OF EVE YET.
YEAH. MAYBE SHE DIDN'T GET OUR MESSAGE.
NOPE, JUST RUNNING A LITTLE BEHIND.

SORRY, FELLAS!
SPACE TRAFFIC WAS A MESS!

THAT'S NEVER HAPPENED TO US BEFORE!
WE'RE ALWAYS ON TIME!

I THINK YOU MEAN "HARDLY EVER" ON TIME.

HA HA HA HA

EXIT
MAN, I'VE ALWAYS WANTED TO DELIVER TO A DUNGEON!

IT'S TRUE. HE HAS.

I CAN'T SAY I'M MUCH FOR DUNGEONS, BUT IF I *DO* HAVE TO BE IN ONE, I'M GLAD IT'S WITH YOU FELLAS.

IMAGINE THE ADVENTURES THAT WERE HAD IN THIS PLACE.

WHOA. WHO IS THAT UP AHEAD?
ONLY ONE WAY TO FIND OUT.

HI!
HELLO!
GLAD TO MEET YOU.

AND NOW I MUST ASK THE SAME QUESTION THAT I HAVE ASKED FOR CENTURIES...
WHAT IS YOUR BUSINESS HERE?

WE'VE COME FROM A FARAWAY LAND TO DELIVER A PACKAGE FROM MISS MANE TO MR. AUGUSTUS.

WELL MET! A STRONG ANSWER. AND THAT IS TO BE ADMIRED.
EVEN SO, THERE IS MORE TO BE ASKED.
BEFORE I LET YOU THROUGH, YOU MUST ANSWER ME THIS.

WHEN IS A TIME WHEN YOU HAVE BEEN MORE THAN THE SUM OF YOUR PARTS?
MAN, THAT'S A TOUGH ONE.
YOU GOT THIS, PAL.
MORE THAN THE SUM OF MY...
HMM...
WAIT!
I KNOW!

IT'S GOTTA BE WHEN I'M WITH THIS GUY!
THE SKILLS THAT WE HAVE COMBINE TO MAKE SOMETHING MUCH BETTER THAN EITHER OF US ARE APART!
IT'S TRUE.

WELL ANSWERED, YOUNG TRAVELER!
I LOVE IT. THANKS FOR SHARING!

SO, WAS THIS, LIKE, SOME SORT OF RIDDLE WE HAD TO SOLVE BEFORE WE COULD PASS?

HA! NO, IT'S NOTHING LIKE THAT.

I'VE BEEN DOWN HERE FOR CENTURIES NOW.
IT IS AN HONOR TO PROTECT THIS PLACE, BUT IT IS A SOLITARY JOB.
WHEN I MEET NEW FRIENDS, I LIKE TO WRITE THEIR STORIES IN THESE BOOKS.

"THEN I READ THEM WHEN I GET LONELY.
"THE NEXT TIME I SEE THEM, IT'S LIKE THEY NEVER LEFT!"

AND WE GET TO BE IN THAT BOOK WITH THEM? SO COOL!

WAIT A SEC...
DID YOU SAY "CENTURIES"?

I CERTAINLY DID.
I BET IT'S BEEN FOREVER SINCE YOU'VE HAD A REALLY GREAT SANDWICH, HUH?

YOU'RE RIGHT.
ACTUALLY, THERE ISN'T MUCH OF ANYTHING THAT'S "REALLY GREAT" IN THE VENDING MACHINES HERE.

THEN YOU'VE GOT TO TRY THIS EGG SALAD SANDWICH THAT KENSIE PUT TOGETHER.
HE'S A SANDWICH GENIUS!

I CONCUR! LEAVE IT TO A COURRIER SERVICE TO MAKE A SANDWICH THAT DELIVERS!
YOU THREE ARE ACES! I'LL BE WISHING BLESSINGS UPON YOU AS YOU CONTINUE YOUR JOURNEY!

AND WITH THOSE SWEET WORDS RINGING IN THEIR EARS, THE TRAVELERS STARTED THE NEXT STAGE OF THEIR JOURNEY.

HEY, EVE?

REMEMBER WHEN OUR NEW FRIEND SAID THAT WHEN HE SEES HIS FARAWAY FRIENDS, IT'S LIKE THEY NEVER LEFT?

YEP!

THAT'S HOW I FEEL WHEN YOU'RE AROUND.

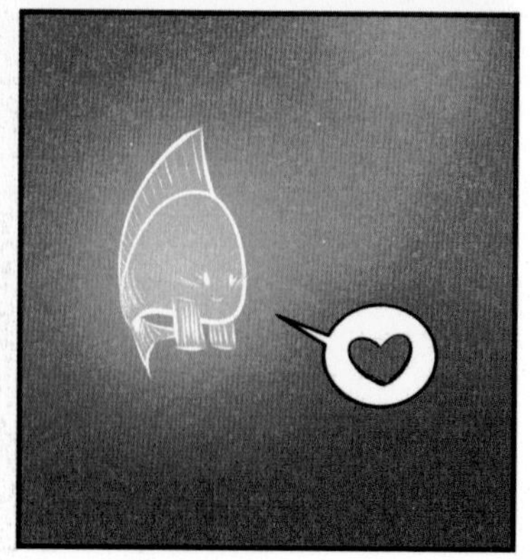

HEY, WHAT'S THAT ON THE WALL UP AHEAD?
LOOKS LIKE A NOTE.

"IF YOU EVER WISH TO LEAVE THE FOLLOWING ROOM, DO NOT GET CAUGHT BY BRUTANIS!"
WHAT DO YOU SUPPOSE IT MEANS?

I DON'T KNOW. GUESS WE'LL JUST HAVE TO PLAY IT BY EAR.

HA! SPOKEN LIKE SOMEONE WHO HAS NEVER LEARNED TO READ SHEET MUSIC.

GUILTY AS CHARGED!

WELL, PLAYING IT BY EAR GOT US IN THE ROOM...
BUT THAT MUST BE BRUTANIS! HOW DO WE GET PAST HER?

I THINK WE'VE GOT THIS.
HOW 'BOUT YOU, KENS?
YEP!

SO WE'RE JUST GOING TO TRY AND SNEAK ACROSS?
YEP!

S'THAT WORK FOR YOU?
YOU KNOW I'M GOOD FOR ANY-THING AS LONG AS IT'S NOT HEIGHTS.

ALL RIGHT! TIME FOR SOME ADVENTURE!

QUICK!
LISTEN, WE'RE DOING ALL RIGHT, BUT SHE'S GOT THAT DOOR COVERED.

I KNOW WHAT YOU MEAN, BUD.
I'VE BEEN WAITING MY WHOLE LIFE TO SAY THESE WORDS...

I THINK WE'RE GOING TO NEED A DISTRACTION!

DID SOMEONE SAY "DISTRACTION"?

OH NO!

WE'RE BUSTED!

WE'LL NEVER LEAVE THIS ROOM AGAIN!

WHAT?
OH! YOU CAN DEFINITELY LEAVE THE ROOM ANY TIME YOU WANT...
AFTER WE SIT DOWN AND HAVE A CHAT!

THANK YOU FOR AGREEING TO SIT DOWN WITH ME.
IT'S NOT OFTEN THAT I GET TO TALK WITH ANYONE OUTSIDE OF MY FELLOW GUARDIANS.
MEETING NEW PEOPLE IS ONE OF THE JOYS OF OUR JOB!

IT'S NICE TO MEET SOMEONE WHO UNDERSTANDS THAT THERE IS JOY TO BE FOUND IN THEIR WORK.
I, TOO, FIND JOY IN MINE. BUT ALSO SOME BITTERNESS.
YOU SEE, I AM FAR FROM HOME...
I RARELY SEE MY FAMILY DUE TO THIS WORK.
AWW.

IT'S NOT ALL CAUSE FOR SADNESS, YOU KNOW.
THIS IS THE ONLY JOB I'VE EVER WANTED.

"AS A CHILD, ALL I DID WAS READ ABOUT PLACES JUST LIKE THIS.
"IT'S ALL I COULD EVER THINK ABOUT.

"AND THE FIRST TIME I SAW ONE IN PERSON?
"IT'S THE CLOSEST THING I'VE FOUND TO MAGIC.

THERE ISN'T A DOUBT IN MY MIND THAT THIS IS WHERE I WAS MEANT TO BE.
EVERY DAY DOING THIS JOB IS THE VERY BEST BLESSING.

THE ONLY BUMMER IS THAT THERE ISN'T MUCH CAUSE FOR THE POST OFFICE TO COME THROUGH THIS NECK OF THE WOODS...
WHICH MAKES IT REALLY HARD TO LET MY FARAWAY FRIENDS KNOW WHEN I'M THINKING OF THEM.

HENCE THE BITTER WITH THE SWEET.
WE'VE HEARD ABOUT THE POST OFFICE SITUATION.
THAT'S GOT TO BE TOUGH.

HEY, POIKO, DO YOU THINK MAYBE WE OUGHT TO JUST LET HER HAVE THE SPARE THING WE KEEP AT THE BOTTOM OF THE BAG?

I DO THINK THAT. LET'S DO IT!

THIS IS A **SHELL PHONE**. THEY ARE PRETTY COMMON WHERE WE COME FROM.
YOU CAN USE IT TO TALK TO ANYONE, ANY-WHERE!
YOU CAN HAVE IT!

ANY-WHERE?
OUT OF THE DUNGEON EVEN?

YOU BET!
THAT'S HOW WE TALK TO EVE, AND SHE LIVES IN **SPACE**!
IT'S TRUE!

AND YOU'RE SAYING THAT I CAN HAVE THIS?
ARE YOU SURE? THIS SEEMS LIKE A PRETTY BIG GIFT.

I'M SURE!
WE'RE GLAD TO DO IT!

THIS IS AMAZING!
THANK YOU SO, SO MUCH! I CAN'T WAIT TO CALL MY FAMILY!

HEY, MOM. IT'S ME!
WHOA. SHE WASN'T LYING. SHE REALLY COULDN'T WAIT.

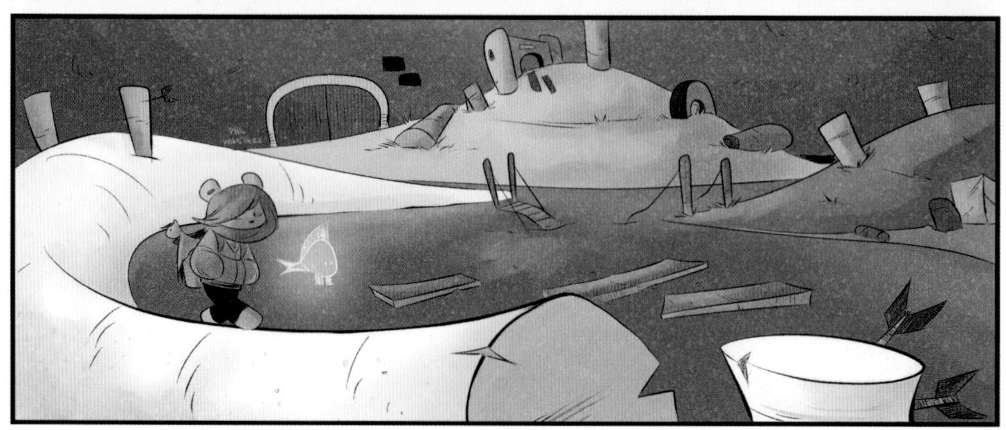

IT'S LOOKING DARK UP AHEAD.
YEAH, BUT I SEE FIREFLIES.
THEY'LL LIGHT THE WAY.

UH-OH...

WE RAN OUT OF FIREFLIES.

IT'S A BIG ROOM, EVE.
YOU GOT THIS?

I THINK SO...

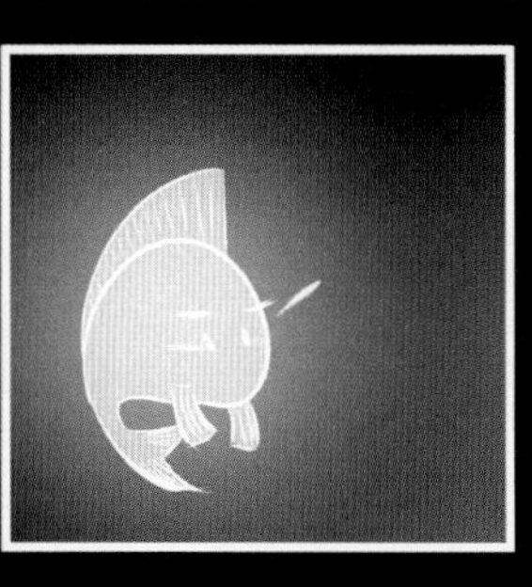

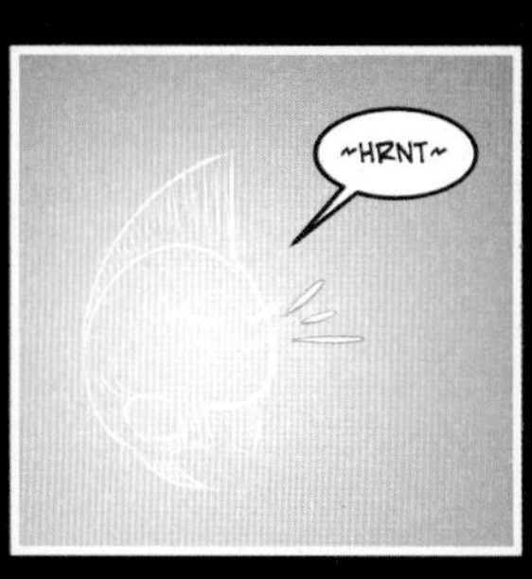
~HRNT~

EVE! THAT WAS SO AWESOME!
IT REALLY WAS.

I'M SO GLAD YOU CAME ALONG ON THIS TRIP!
WHENEVER YOU NEED ME, POIKO, I'M THERE!

THIS LOOKS LIKE THE PLACE.
AUGUSTUS
TIME TO MAKE A DELIVERY.

WHO'S THERE?
IT'S POIKO. WE HAVE A DELIVERY FOR AUGUSTUS.

ARE WE DELIVERING TO A STACK OF BOOKS?
WOULDN'T BE THE FIRST TIME!

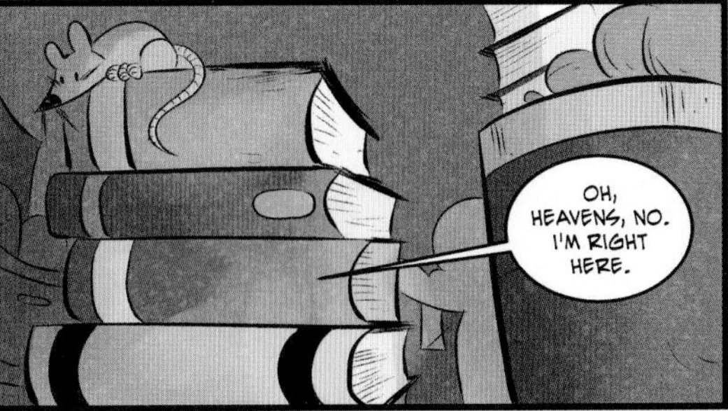
OH, HEAVENS, NO. I'M RIGHT HERE.

ER... HERE.

THIS IS FOR YOU!

AN ENVELOPE?

AND IT SMELLS LIKE...
MISS MANE?

OH!
AWESOME.

WHEN I WAS A MUCH YOUNGER NEWT, I USED TO BE IN A SKA PUNK BAND WITH MISS MANE.
WE WERE CALLED **AUGUSTUS AND THE MANE THING.**

I HAVEN'T SEEN HER IN, OH, I'D SAY ABOUT TWENTY YEARS.
BUT WE STILL KEEP IN TOUCH.

AND YOU STILL CONSIDER HER A FRIEND EVEN THOUGH YOU HAVEN'T SEEN HER IN SO LONG?

FOR SURE!
FRIENDSHIP ISN'T ABOUT THE QUANTITY OF TIME SPENT TOGETHER.
IT'S ABOUT THE ***QUALITY*** OF THAT TIME AND THE MEMORIES YOU'VE MADE TOGETHER.

AND FROM WHAT I CAN TELL, YOU THREE HAVE THAT IN SPADES!
YOU KNOW WHAT?

I THINK SO, TOO!

AND WITH THEIR DELIVERY COMPLETE, THE TRIO HEADS FOR THE DOOR.

WELL, THE JOB IS ABOUT DONE, NOW.
WE'RE GOING TO MISS YOU, EVE.
IT'S TRUE. IT'S A BUMMER WHEN YOU'RE GONE.
I FEEL THE SAME WAY.
CUZ WE'RE FRIENDS?
FOREVER.

DUNGEON
IT'S ALWAYS THE LAST LEG OF THE JOURNEY THAT FEELS MOST BITTER-SWEET.
IT ALWAYS COMES UP TOO SOON.
I AGREE.

WITH THE JOB COMPLETED, EVE RETURNED TO THE STARS.
SEE YOU SOON, FELLAS!
BYE, EVE!

WHAT A GREAT DAY, RIGHT?
FOR SURE!
DO YOU EVER THINK THERE WILL BE A DAY WHERE THE JOB ISN'T AS FUN?

WITH YOU BY MY SIDE?

NOT A CHANCE!
FIN.

BONUS STUFF

BRIAN MIDDLETON

has been telling stories in one form or another for his whole life. His first comic book (published by his brother's 4th grade teacher and the school's copy machine) sold out at the distributor level. After that, there was no looking back! After dipping his toe in the water with a handful of self-published and work-for-hire comics, he decided to take the deep dive and create his first series, *Wulfborne*, at Scout Comics. He then turned his creative attention toward this project, *Poiko: Quests & Stuff*. The rest of his attention is focused squarely on his one wonderful wife, two beautiful daughters, and six (*feel free, dear reader, to fill in here the adjective of your choice*) cats.

Eve's
SCRAPBOOK
—by Eve—

MISS MANE'S SET LIST!

REUNION SET:

01. BLUEPRINTS (FOR A BETTER TOMORROW)
02. SONG OF MY HEART
03. PUNK ALL DAY (AND SLEEP ALL NIGHT)

04. NEW SONG "CAN'T WAIT" "WHITE PICKET FENCES AND SIDE WALKS MADE OF GOLD."

(DRUM SOLO)

05. HERE AND THERE
06. GOODBYE
* NO BREAK
07. BRAND NEW DAY
08. TOMORROW DON'T COME (CHEAP)

(INTRODUCE BAND MEMBERS) DON'T FORGET ACHILLES!

09. OTHER NEW ONE ← AGF AGF AGF CG
10. SYNONYM
11. RIGHT WHEN YOU SAID IT * CUT IF SET IS RUNNING LONG!
12. THE END (FOR NOW)

ENCORE: UNITE!

MUSIC IS GOOD FOR the SOUL

AUGUSTUS' PICK!

AUGUSTUS&THE
MANE_THING

SEC 6 *
ROW 02

FRI 8:00PM

NO REFUND
NO EXCHANGE

ACHILLES & AUGUSTUS

MISS MANE!

A REPRODUCTION OF A PHOTO TAKEN BY PIERRE, THE WORLD'S PREMIER POET, DURING ONE OF HIS MANY JOURNEYS.
A DRAWING MADE BY POIKO, BASED ON PIERRE'S PICTURE.

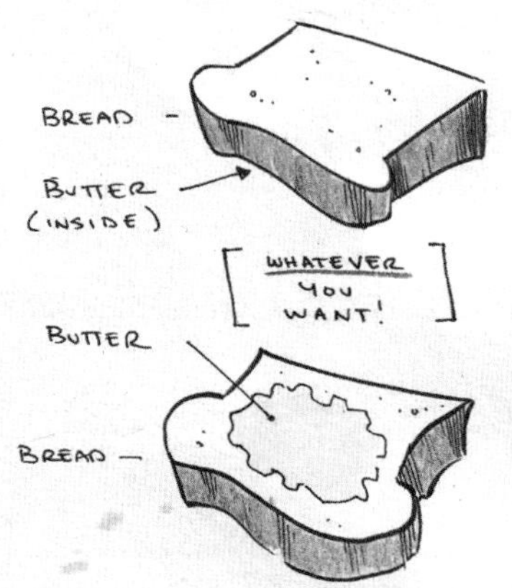

A SANDWICH A day...

TESTIMONIALS

"THIS SANDWICH IS TO DIE FOR. TRUST ME."
-OLD PHIL RIVERMAN

"I EAT KENSIE'S SANDWICHES EVERY DAY OF THE WEEK. SOMETIMES I HAVE THEM FOR BREAKFAST. OKAY, MOST TIMES. OKAY, YEAH, I EAT THEM FOR BREAKFAST EVERY DAY."

-ANONYMOUS LOCAL DELIVERY PERSON

A PHOTO OF A FELLOW ADVENTURER.

A PHOTO OF PIERRE WHEN HE WAS JUST A YOUNG POET.

A PANEL FROM POIKO'S COMIC, "THE LION WITH THE LIGHTNING SWORD."

JUST SOME RANDOM STUFF

A SILLY CARTOON ABOUT VIOLETTE'S DAD.